The Dirty Little Boy

Margaret Wise Brown
Illustrated by Steven Salerno

Marshall Cavendish Children

O ne day, a little boy came to his big round mother,
and he said: "Mother, I am one dirty little boy.
I have jam on my face and chocolate on my knee.
I have mud all over my feet and between my toes from

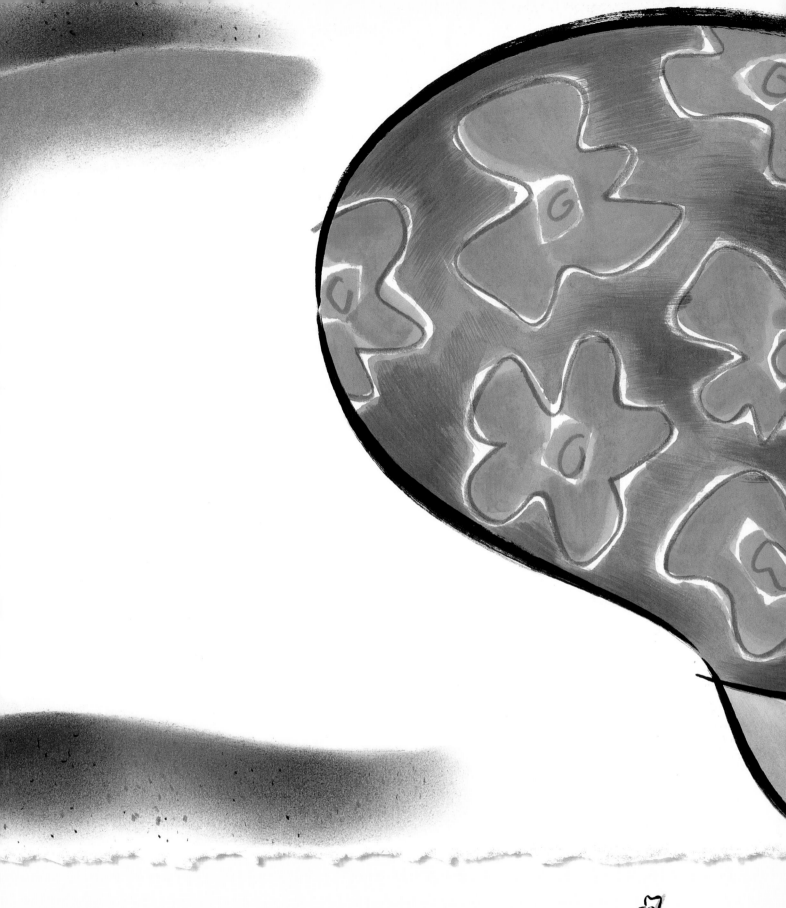

walking down the wet, muddy road. I have dust in my hair from the wind blowing yesterday, and I just have dirt all over me.

"I think I want to take a bath."

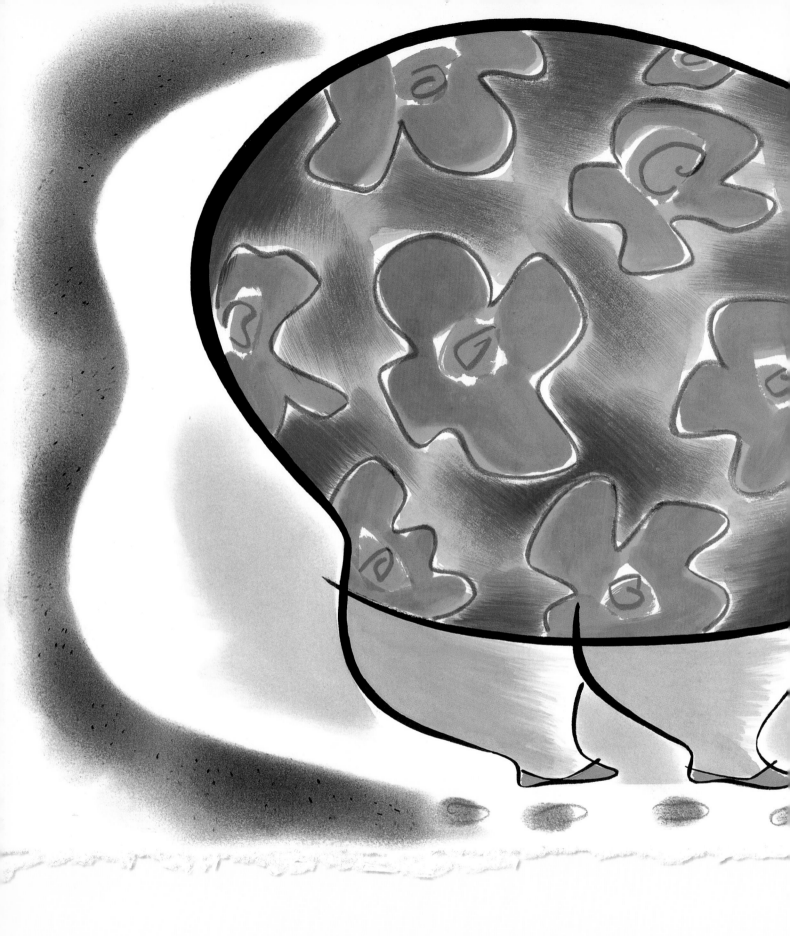

"Well, little boy," said his big round mother, "I am so busy scrubbing white clothes that I can't give you a bath right this second. Run along, and see how the animals take their baths and that way you'll learn how to get clean."

So the little boy started down the road to see how the animals took a bath. Soon he came to a little bird sitting on the branch of a tree.

"Little bird," said the boy, "I want to take a bath, only I don't know how. So I have come to watch you take a bath."

The little bird began to flutter and ruffle up its feathers. It flew off the tree and dove straight into the mud puddle. It hopped around the edge a little. Then, stomach first, it

sank into the shallow part of the puddle and shook itself
so that water splashed all over its back and wings. It
hopped out on the sand in the road and shook some
more. It flapped its wings. *Whirrrr.*

It shook and shook itself again and bent its head and
smoothed out its feathers and then it flew away.

"So!" thought the little boy, "this is the way to take a bath." And he ran out in the middle of the road and lay on his stomach in the mud puddle. He wiggled about, and he splashed the muddy water all over himself. Then he got out and rolled in the sand by the side of the road.

But when he got up, he was dirtier than ever.

"Oh, dear," said the little boy, "I'm dirtier than I was before. I guess little boys just don't take baths like birds. I guess I had better go on down the road and find some other animals."

So he walked on down the road until he came to a
farm. There by the side of the road was a farmer's pigpen
with six dirty little pigs in it and a big black pool of water.

"Shoo, little pigs, take a bath," shouted the boy.
"Shoo, little pigs, take a bath so that this dirty little boy
can learn how to get clean."

Just then, two of the little pigs went into the pool
and wallowed about in its black edges. The boy didn't
even wait for them to come out. He jumped the fence
and got right into the black, muddy pool and rolled
around squealing with the little pigs. The water and mud
was so cool and soft, the boy was sure that this was the

only way to take a bath. But when he got out he was dirtier than ever. He was all covered and black and sticky with mud.

"Oh, dear," said the little boy, "this must not be the way for a boy to take a bath," and he walked on down the road, dirtier than he had ever been before.

After a while he came to a small white house.
There on the front porch sat an old yellow cat, licking
her paw and brushing her wet paw against the side of
her face. The boy stood and watched her. Then he licked
his hand and rubbed it on his cheek, and licked his other

hand and rubbed it on his ear and licked his hand and
rubbed it on his neck. His hands were getting cleaner.

"Oh, shucks," said the boy, "this sure is the way
to take a bath."

Through the doorway of the small white house, he saw a mirror hanging in the hall and he ran to look at his face. But in the mirror his face was dirtier than it had ever been before. He had rubbed all the dirt off his hands and onto his face.

"Oh, dear," said the boy as he ran down the road. "I washed like a bird and I washed like a pig and I washed like a cat, and I'm dirtier than I ever was before. How will I ever learn to take a bath and be a clean little boy?"

Way down the road he came to a green field with
brown shining horses galloping and frisking about in the
sunshine. He had never seen such smooth shining horses.
And beyond the green field with the shining horses was
a big white barn.

"Those horses are certainly clean," thought
the little boy, "clean and shining." And he wished
that he was clean and shining and running about
in the green fields.

He went up to the big white barn and stood in the doorway. Two men with brushes were cleaning a horse. The brushes made *scrape, shsh, scrape, shsh* noises in the

horse's coat. The little boy watched them. He watched them stir the brush around the horse's coat until all the gray dirt and dust came out of the hair.

He watched them take a yellow shiny bristle brush
and brush away all the dirt that the iron brush had stirred
up. There the horse stood, smooth and brown and clean.
And he watched them lead the horse out of the stable
and into the field. As soon as they were out of sight, he
grabbed the sharp iron brush and he rubbed it over one of

his muddy legs. Ouch! The sharp ends scratched
him and just made white lines in the dirt on his leg.
"Oh, dear, what shall I do?" said the little boy.
"I've washed like a bird, and I've washed like a pig.
I've washed like a cat, and I've washed like a horse,
and still the dirt will not come off."

So the little boy went back to his big round mother, dirtier than he had ever been before. His mother was just pulling the last piece of white clothes out of the big soapy tub of water when her little boy came home.

"I declare, little boy," she said, "you are dirtier than I have ever seen you before. Didn't you learn from the animals how to get clean?"

"I washed like a bird, and I washed like a pig. I washed like a cat, and I washed like a horse, Mother, and each time I just got a little bit dirtier than I had ever been before."

"You are no bird, little boy, you are no pig, you are no cat, and you are no horse. How is it that you didn't figure that out? How is it that you didn't find out how little boys take a bath?"

And she turned on the water and grabbed him by the back of his neck and put him right into the big soapy tub.

"I guess it's your mother who will have to show
you how to get clean." And so she scrubbed him and
scrubbed him all slippery with soap. And when he came
out of his mother's tub, he was cleaner than a bird, he

was cleaner than a pig, he was cleaner than a cat.
And he was cleaner than a horse.
He was clean and shining,
like a clean little boy.

For Grandma Rose
S.S.

This story was originally called "How the Animals Took a Bath." It was first published in *Jack and Jill* magazine in 1939. Later, in 1957, it appeared in a story collection published by Curtis Publishing Company. This version has a few slight changes from the original that were approved by Margaret Wise Brown's estate.

Text copyright © 2001 by Margaret Wise Brown
Illustration copyright © 2001 by Steven Salerno
Marshall Cavendish Corporation, 99 White Plains Road, Tarrytown, NY 10591
www.marshallcavendish.us

Library of Congress Cataloging-in-Publication Data

Brown, Margaret Wise, 1910–1952.
The dirty little boy / by Margaret Wise Brown ; illustrated by Steven Salerno.— 1st Marshall Cavendish paperback ed.
p. cm.
Summary: When a little boy tries to get clean the way different animals do, he only gets dirtier.
ISBN 0-7614-5180-3
[1. Cleanliness—Fiction. 2. Baths—Fiction. 3. Animals—Fiction.] I. Salerno, Steven, ill. II. Title.

PZ7.B8163Di 2004
[Fic]—dc22
2003022116

Creative director: Bretton Clark
Designer: Billy Kelly
Editor: Margery Cuyler

The illustrations in this book were prepared with mixed media.

Printed in China

First Marshall Cavendish paperback edition, 2005
Reprinted by arrangement with WinslowHouse International, Inc.

2 4 6 8 10 9 7 5 3 1